The First Spell of Winnefred Broomstock

By Peter G. Blank

Illustrated by Thomas Sperling

Checkerboard Press ❖ New York

Text ©1992 Peter G. Blank. Illustrations ©1992 Checkerboard Press, Inc., 30 Vesey Street, New York, New York, 10007. All rights reserved.
ISBN: 1-56288-273-2 Library of Congress Catalog Card Number: 92-71150 Printed in the U.S.A. F(1/14) 0 9 8 7 6 5 4 3 2 1

Halloween was almost here and Winnefred Broomstock hadn't yet decided what costume she would wear to the witches' ball that night. Having just turned seven, this was her first ball, and she wanted her costume to be extra special.

Making a decision wasn't easy. Ordinary children can buy or rent or have their mothers make their costumes. But first-year witches must conjure their costumes from thin air, and the spell they use has to be just right.

For many months, all the littlest witches had been going to the library and searching through the great books of incantations, spells, and magic to find just the right ingredients for their Hallows' Eve costumes. And Winnefred, or "Whisk," as her friends called her because her broom was so small, was no different.

She had spent hours paging through book after book, looking for just the right words to cast her spell. Sometimes there were so many books on her table that only the crooked point of her slightly too large witch's hat could be seen frantically moving up and down and side to side as she paged through the books. Every so often she would stop and write something down on the pad of paper at her side, pause for a moment, giggle to herself, and then pick up another book.

The clock on the library wall said that it would soon be closing time. The old warlock who sat at the front desk had already begun to turn off the lights when Winnefred suddenly jumped up from her chair.

"I've got it!" she proclaimed, waving the single sheet of paper that contained all her scribblings and notes high above her head. The old warlock looked sternly at the commotion as the other little witches ran to her side. "Read it! Read it!" they all clamored.

Winnefred paused a moment, waiting for them to settle down. Then, slowly, like a spider weaving a web, she began to recite the spell she had written:

"If giggling Ghost perchance you see,
Unlock it with a Skeleton Key,
Then fly with Feather from sleeping owl,
Past moonshine full and Wolfen Howl,
Upon a broom of whiskers Cat,
All mixed within a Sorcerer's Hat,
Then spice it with the tail of Toad,
And Lizard's tongue and Spider cold,
Now add a bit of cross-eyed Bat,
A sprinkle of This, a touch of That,
And pour into a Pumpkin gold,
For this is how a spell is told."

All the little witches stood silent and motionless, clinging to every word of the incantation. Even the old warlock stood still. Listening from the back of the library, he seemed to be caught in the spell.

"Repeat. Repeat. Repeat this rhyme," Winnefred continued, her voice now just a whisper. "Repeat. Repeat for one more time…

"Then spin on foot and turn thrice round,
And step-step back and forward bound,
Now close your eyes and count one, two,
And see your hallow'd spell come…

"TRUE!" she shouted.

The startled little witches jumped, then burst into a chorus of laughter. But before they could say anything, the old warlock announced,

"The time is nigh for all to leave,
The witching hour is here.
Go home, go home,
On broomsticks fly
And dream of Halloween cheer."

As all the little witches scurried home to collect their costumes for the ball, the clock on the library wall began to chime, "Begone, begone, begone…"

The old warlock stood at the door, waiting for the last little witch to pass. Winnefred, the littlest, as usual was straggling behind, trying to collect her things. As the old warlock began to close the door behind her, she suddenly stopped and said, "Wait, I forgot my broom!"

Winnefred pushed the door open and rushed past the warlock. She quickly grabbed the little broom, which she had left beside her chair. Then, turning around to leave, she was suddenly stopped by the old warlock, who was now standing in her path.

"It's a good spell, Whisk," he said, a broad smile covering his face. "You might just win the contest for the scariest costume."

"You really think so?" She asked.

The old warlock nodded.

"Hmmm," she said, now heading out the door, "scariest costume…I wonder."

As the old warlock closed the door behind her, the town hall clock reminded Winnefred that time was running out. "The witches' ball will soon be starting," she thought, "and I still have a lot of work to do. I must make a list."

Winnefred sat down on the library steps, just below the gargoyle that was perched atop the door. She pulled out her writing pad from the sack she used to carry her books.

"Let's see," she thought, "first I'll need a…" Winnefred began writing down the ingredients she required. Every so often she would pause to check her notes on the piece of paper that contained the incantation. Her face was filled with concentration. Her tongue, now firmly placed in a thinking position at one corner of her mouth, seemed to mirror each stroke of the pencil as she wrote down the items.

1. A Sorcerer's HAT, with STAR and MOON
2. A Scraggly CAT, with whiskers broom
3. A SPIDER COLD that has turned BLUE
4. A GHOST that laughs instead of "BOO!"
5. A Skeleton KEY from finger hung
6. A LIZARD with a SPOTTED TONGUE
7. The FEATHER of a sleeping owl
8. A cross-eyed BAT from Wolfen HOWL
9. A TOAD with TAIL is HARD To FIND
10. A PUMPKIN with a golden rind

"There, that's everything I need," she said as she tore the page from the pad and inspected her work. Checking it over one last time, Winnefred asked herself, "Now where do I begin?"

"At the beginning," a little voice beside her head said.

Winnefred spun around to see who was there, only to find the gargoyle looking over her shoulder.

"What's it going to be?" the inquisitive gargoyle asked.

Winnefred stood, gathered up her belongings, and began to walk down the steps. When she got to the sidewalk, she turned back to the gargoyle and said, "You'll see."

She turned around once more, took the handle of the rickety old wagon that was tucked beneath the steps, and started down the street to collect the ingredients for her incantation.

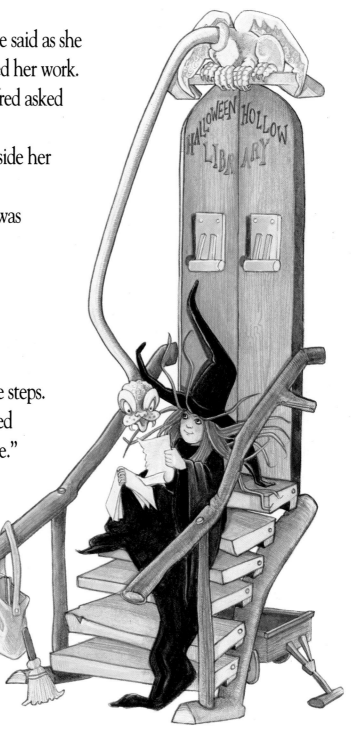

A Sorcerer's HAT,
with STAR and MOON

A Scraggly CAT, with whiskers broom

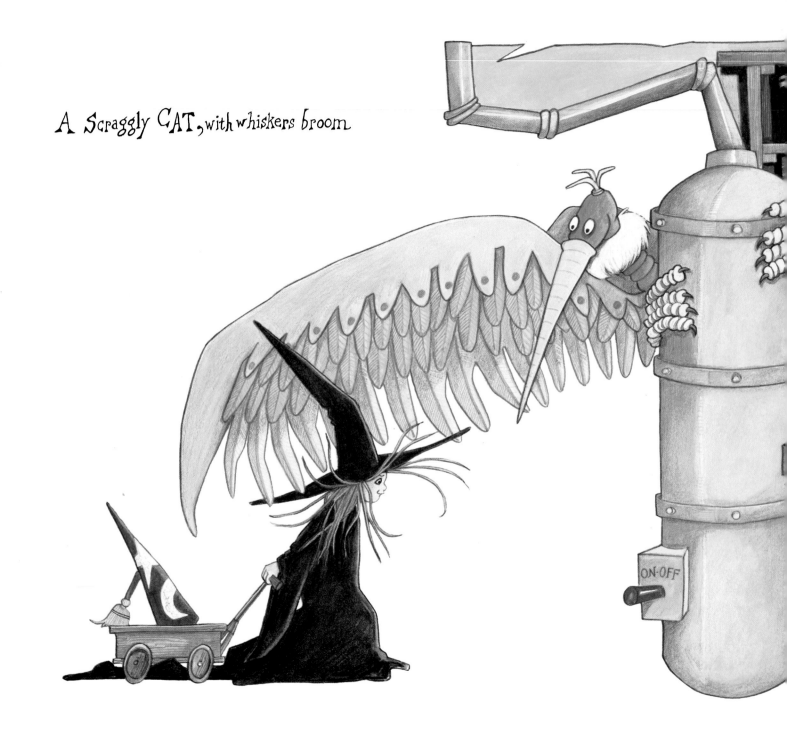

A SPIDER COLD that has turned BLUE

A *GHOST* that laughs
instead of *"BOO!"*

A Skeleton KEY
from finger hung

SLEEP TIGHT, DON'T LET THE BEDBUGS BITE
CEMETERY

A LIZARD with a SPOTTED TONGUE

The FEATHER of a sleeping owl

A cross-eyed BAT
from Wolfen HOWL

A TOAD with TAIL IS HARD TO FIND

A PUMPKIN with a golden rind

PROPERTY OF
ICHABOD SCARECROW
TOWN FARMER

The town hall clock had just begun to strike midnight when Winnefred arrived at the witches' ball, pulling her wagon, which was now filled with all the things that she needed to conjure up her costume. All the other witches, the old warlock, and even the gargoyle were already in their costumes. Winnefred began to slowly assemble the ingredients for her incantation. The room grew still.

First she turned the sorcerer's hat upside down. Then, reciting the incantation under her breath, Winnefred began to place the items one by one into the hat.

"…Then spice it with the tail of Toad
And Lizard's tongue and Spider cold,
Now add a bit of cross-eyed Bat,
A sprinkle of—"

She stopped. Everyone gasped, "Has she forgotten the spell?"

Winnefred reached into her sack and
pulled out the small pencil sharpener
she used to keep her pencil sharp.
Emptying it into the hat, she continued,

"A sprinkle of This, a touch of That,
And pour into a Pumpkin gold,
For this is how a spell is told."

Winnefred poured the contents of the hat
into the pumpkin and repeated the spell five more times. She spun around on one foot
until she had completed three turns. Then she took two steps back and leapt forward,
landing right in front of the old warlock. He winked at her as she spoke the final words of
the incantation.

"Now close your eyes and count one, two,
And see your hallow'd spell come true!"

With a flash of light and a magical puff,
the room was suddenly filled with smoke. When
the smoke cleared, there, standing in the middle
of the room, was Winnefred wearing her costume.
"Aarrrgh! How horrible!" the witches screamed.
"How frightening!"

For Winnefred had conjured
up the scariest costume of all.